THOUGHTS XVI:

Assemblage Points:
Defining Energies

©Herb Stevenson 2026

CONTENTS

Thoughts XVI:
Assemblage Points:

Defining Energies

Healing Den Publishing Company

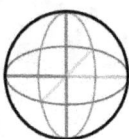

Preface

This is the sixteenth of an unknown number of volumes of Thoughts, a journey of self-discovery and revelation of many of life's mysteries that seek understanding and integration into the collective human mind. The process is somewhat whimsical as true learning often requires one's world view to be bent, twisted, or broken so as to frame break habitualized thinking that prevents one from realizing their actual existence in the co-creating world.

In this story we explore the assemblage point, described by Carlos Castenada[1] Through different exercises in shifting awareness, Carlos was able to "see" energy and to understand "reality" – as we experience it. By altering awareness to different vantage-points, a person can be made to see that our version of "reality" is simply another dream – a dream that has been made solid by a lifetime of intent, conditioning and training, and it is no more real or valid than other worlds and other realities that practitioners are trained to access, simply by shifting the "valve of consciousness" that forces the interpretation of "reality". This "valve of consciousness" is called "the assemblage point".[2]

The journey thus far in the fifteen prior volumes has led to the question of what is real while seeking to provide existential roadmaps (experiential constructs) to support those that follow his journey. In this episode, we begin to examine a deeper perspective by looking at evolutionary energies designed to expand awareness through fragmenting old and/or developing new levels of consciousness much like the combining of one bubble of conscious into another to form an expanded form of consciousness. This expanding reframes the prior consciousness into a new form of consciousness that is more than the sum of its prior parts.

Synopsis of Key Points in the book

The key learning points are:

- **Assemblage Point Concept**: The assemblage point, as

described by Carlos Castaneda, is a focal point of energy that influences our perception of reality. Shifting this point can alter our awareness and perception, revealing that our version of reality is just one of many possible interpretations.

- **Reality and Consciousness**: The document explores the idea that reality is shaped by our intent, conditioning, and training. By altering our awareness, we can access different dimensions and realities.

- **Evolution of Consciousness**: The journey of self-discovery involves expanding awareness by integrating new levels of consciousness, much like combining bubbles to form a larger one. This process reframes prior consciousness into a more comprehensive form.

- **Role of Energy and Frequency**: Thoughts and feelings are forms of energy with specific frequencies. Higher frequencies lead to higher levels of awareness and the dissolution of lower frequency beliefs and emotions.

- **Free Will and Programming**: The concept of free will is discussed in the context of pre-existing programming and imprints. True free will involves developing conscious awareness and internal authority to transcend these limitations.

- **Time Crystals**: Moments frozen in time, referred to as time crystals, are part of our energetic field and can form clusters. These need to be dissolved for higher awareness and healing.

- **Integration and Awakening**: The process of awakening involves dissolving old beliefs and programming, leading to a higher frequency of conscious awareness. This is facilitated by practices like meditation and the development of internal authority.

- **Desire and Intent**: Desire and intent play crucial roles in the awakening process. They can be unconscious or conscious and influence the manifestation of reality.

- **Guided Meditation**: The document includes a guided meditation to help participants experience and understand the concepts discussed, particularly the dissolution of time crystals and the shifting of the assemblage point.

- **Holistic Understanding**: The overall message emphasizes the importance of holistic understanding and the integration of various experiences and insights to achieve a higher state of consciousness and presence.

These points collectively highlight the journey of expanding consciousness, the role of energy and perception, and the importance of internal authority and intentionality in shaping our reality.

Acknowledgements

As I continue to listen to the many voices of the past that have impacted my life and thinking, I extend a deep sense of gratitude to Rudy Bauer and his unending writing on existentialism and phenomenology, Edwin Nevis, Frances Baker, John Carter and Claire for their support in learning gestalt theory and therapy, Carlos Castenda and Eduardo Duran for their spiritual novels. I am sure there are many others that I do not remember in this moment.

A deep sense of gratitude to Mary Lynne Princic for reading and commenting on each book.

Sincere and deep gratitude to Hannah Princic-Lowe for editing and getting each book published. Your infectious smile and encouragement have been invaluable.

A Note

We are all on a journey, unique to only ourself. As you explore your inner world, allow your internal authority to reveal the even grander world that exists beyond your present beliefs. As you do so, the suffering of day-to-day life melts away and you just might find your true self.

Bountiful blessings

Herb Stevenson

PS: if you find these books useful, pass it on to a friend.

Forward

This book does not ask to be read so much as entered.

Thoughts XVI: Assemblage Points – Defining Energies continues a long and deliberate journey into the subtle terrain where perception, meaning, and awareness intersect. What unfolds in these pages is not a doctrine, nor a system demanding belief, but an invitation to notice how reality is assembled—moment by moment—through attention, energy, and consciousness itself.

Herb Stevenson writes from a place that is both disciplined and compassionate. The ideas explored here—assemblage points, shifting awareness, time crystals, and the evolution of consciousness—are presented not as abstractions, but as lived inquiries. They are meant to be felt, reflected upon, and metabolized slowly. The narrative reminds us that understanding does not always arrive linearly; insight often waits patiently until awareness is ready to receive it.

Readers familiar with phenomenology, existential inquiry, or contemplative practice will recognize a deep respect for experience over explanation. Those new to these ideas may find themselves gently unsettled—in the best possible way—as habitual ways of seeing are softened, questioned, and re-formed. This is not disruption for its own sake, but a compassionate loosening of certainty that allows something truer to emerge.

At its core, this work is about remembering—remembering the internal authority that precedes conditioning, remembering that consciousness is not fixed, and remembering that suffering often dissolves not through force, but through awareness. The journey offered here does not promise answers; it offers presence. And presence, as this book quietly demonstrates, is often enough.

May you read these pages with patience, curiosity, and kindness toward yourself. Allow the ideas to unfold in their own time. If something resonates, stay with it. If something confuses you, let it rest. The path described here is not one of urgency, but of attunement—and each reader will find their own assemblage point shifting in precisely the way it needs to.

Hannah Lowe, Ph.D., LPCC-S, NCC

ONE: A NEW DAY

Tom woke to a brisk morning and glistening sunshine. As he grabbed a coffee and headed to see the sunrise, he became breathless. As he peered into the sunlight, it felt like a magical portal was opening and inviting him to come and play. Come and see the world beyond this world. See what is behind all of creation.

Tom was silent as he felt the sunlight permeate every cell in his body and for a moment he felt like he was beaming through the portal. As if startled by a memory imprinted at birth that he is supposed to stay in this world and in this body, he refocused to the morning. The afterglow of the moment continued to fill his body.

He continued to drink coffee until he felt the energy behind him reveal DocKnow was behind him.

"Good morning," said Tom, as he turned to greet his friend.

DocKnow was smiling and holding a full cup of coffee and the coffee pot as he offered a fresh pour to Tom.

"Good morning, it is," said DocKnow. "For a moment I thought you were going to go ahead and walk through the portal the sun was offering."

Tom chuckled and said, "I was definitely leaning towards it before an old imprint exploded reminding that I am supposed to stay here until I awake sufficiently to dissolve the original programming to not explore beyond the bounds of my humanity."

DocKnow laughed and said, "I think it's a little too late for you **as if anyone** has explored way beyond his human programming, **it is you**. I imagine you have some residual beliefs about your being a physical form until you're not, however, you have clearly stretched yourself beyond the bounds of being your body. I daresay, you have done everything to bring your awareness and therefore all of yourself into human experience and beyond."

Tom nodded as he recalled the many experiences beyond day-to-day life that he experienced with DocKnow and the others.

Tom looked into the infinite eyes of DocKnow and said, "I wonder about those that seem to be able to explore......"

"Other dimensions," interrupted White Horse as he walked into the sunroom with an empty coffee cup. Reaching towards DocKnow with his cup, White Horse smiled and nodded for him to pour..

DocKnow smiled and feigned not sharing and then filled White Horse's cup.

All three laughed.

White Horse looked at Tom and said, "sounds like your pondering what Carlos Castenada wrote about 50 years ago."

Tom paused as he recalled having read all of the Castenada books when each was published. Now, in this reflective moment of no time, he recalled that he had consumed each book like a file being downloaded to a computer. More like witnessing himself at those places in time, he suddenly realized that that was what had happened. He had downloaded the information into his brain as if to store it in himself like an organic intelligence that was storing the information until a precise synchronous moment to experience an integrative insight.

DocKnow asked, "it seems you just had an infinite moment?"

Tom sputtered, "maybe."

Tom shared his experience as DocKnow and White Horse listened.

After a bit of silence, DocKnow said, "infinite moments occur when asynchronous[3] information becomes synchronous without any apparent causality except that a new frequency connects the information into an insight or awakening experience."

Tom said, "so my experience with the sunrise and White Horse's reference to Castenada created a resonance with all that was read 50 years ago to create an integrative insight or at least the beginning of one."

"You tell me," said DocKnow.

Tom had to sit for a moment and ponder.

White Horse suggested, "how about we have breakfast and allow this to simmer so I can fill my belly with breakfast burritos."

DocKnow almost knocked White Horse to the ground as he headed for the breakfast burritos.

White Horse and Tom laughed and then realized they had better head for the kitchen.

Crystal Mare was singing in the kitchen as the three of them arrived at the table. Walks with Woman came from the barn having fed the horses.

DocKnow slid into the kitchen to make a fresh pot of coffee and in his most polite voice, he asked Crystal Mare to include jalapeno peppers in at least one burrito.

Crystal Mare smiled and said, "I think you will be happy" as she carried a large plate of burritos to the table.

DocKnow decided to leave the coffee and skipped back to the table, plopping into his chair. As he looked around, he saw everyone holding their coffee cups in the air to avoid spilling.

DocKnow smiled wanly and then beamed as Crystal Mare dropped a large burrito onto to his plate.

Tom noticed refried beans, green peppers, jalapeño peppers and habanero peppers in DocKnow's burrito. He excused himself and went to the kitchen. When he came back, he placed a quart of milk and a fresh pot of coffee in front of DocKnow. The timing was perfect as DocKnow was halfway through the burrito and sweat was pouring from his face.

Tom smiled and sat down. With a deep sense of appreciation for everyone, he placed a burrito on his plate. It was exceptional.

Tom said thanks to Crystal Mare, who said, "White Horse did most of the cooking."

All nodded to him.

TWO: DOWNLOADING

Breakfast was filled with the sounds of enjoyable food and friendship. As they finished eating, DocKnow brought out a bag of bear claws Danish.

Everyone looked at DocKnow as if in wonder at how he seemed to manifest these Danish at will and then realized it was something they would simply enjoy and not waste time wondering.

When the kitchen was filled with clean dishes, they decided to go for a brief walk.

Tom noticed that their walk felt like they were preparing for a conversation without anyone talking. They simply meandered around the property engaging every aspect of the land as if seeking and experiencing it for the first time.

DocKnow suggested "let's head back to the house."

When they arrived, they quietly found coffee or green tea and met at the picnic table in the yard under the warm sun.

In his humorous way, DocKnow smiled at everyone and said, "I think we are fully present."

Everyone nodded, though in a somewhat quizzical way as if wondering is he teasing or is he suggesting that we get present. Regardless, DocKnow seemed to shift the frequency and everyone ready or not was not only present, but fully aware that very high vibrations had surrounded and permeated each of them.

No one said anything.

"I raised the vibration a notch or two as I want us to be able to draw upon moments in our lives that we have ignored and are instrumental in how we have become who we are in this very specific moment," said DocKnow.

Tom thought, 'well that's one way to get our attention.'

DocKnow continued, "I would like to shift our perceptions to times you wondered why you did something even though it felt like it was important in some way that made no sense."

Tom instantly remembered 50 years prior when he was reading books that he did not really understand but seemed important as if he was downloading or inputting information. He was in the US Marines and recalled in detail reading Rollo May and other books that felt important regardless of his understanding....as he did not understand them at all.

DocKnow continued, "these are moments or experiences that somehow became very important at some point in time often many years later. Initially, they may have felt odd and asynchronous to anything in your life only to become deeply insightful to who you are."

Tom continued to recall the readings and how they had become instrumental in his life. When he began to meditate and started his training in Gestalt, he began recalling those readings.

Tom asked, "these moments seemed asynchronous at the time, and are you saying that they were somehow part of our calling to our awakening?"

DocKnow nodded yes.

Everyone looked at DocKnow as if awestruck. One by one, they shared experiences that seemed totally out of character at the time but later were perceptually reframed into a life changing awareness.

Tom noted what he had recalled, "it was 50+ years ago that I was reading Rollo May and a variety of psychology books. At the time I wondered why I was reading them. Twenty years later, I began to recall the content as if it had been sitting in my brain in cold storage until time to re-member. I recall an oddness when remembering as if now I remember the content and wonder how this all happened. It was baffling as I was able to understand existentialism, phenomenology and gestalt in a very confusing experience. I was elated to understand and bewildered at how I was able to understand these concepts. As I reflect on it now, it seems like reading was a form of download of information that I needed to store. Moreover, it is like the brain, or some form of intelligence was processing it in the background asynchronously until a specific conscious awareness developed which then triggered re-membering."

White Horse suggested, "like this morning when I mentioned Carlos Castenada's name to you. Suddenly, it seemed like your recalled the reading 40+ years ago and it opened your eyes to multidimensionality in a new or insightful way."

"Yes, like this morning," said Tom. "Your words reverberated through me reminding me of Castenada's teaching about the assemblage point, multidimensionality and the clearing of imprints[4]. More importantly, it felt like the original reading was more of a story of possibilities and today it felt like the information had been stored until released to connect a series of what seemed asynchronous experiences into a coherent understanding not possible till now."

Crystal Mare was grimacing then said, "this bends my sense of reality as I am realizing that I have had similar experiences as if I am collating and integrating a series of asynchronous events into what I had originally called epiphanies or insights. It never occurred to me that maybe these experiences were guided or imprinted or directed from something beyond my present awareness."

"Like guidance from our higher self," said Walks with Woman.

In an uncoordinated movement, all nodded their agreement.

White Horse asked, "so we are all acknowledging that in our

individual and unique ways, each of us is saying that we have been guided by something beyond ourself as we know it, possibly *our higher self or some other spiritual entity?*"

All nodded their agreement.

THREE: THOUGHTS AND FEELING TONES

They decided to mull over what had been said for a brief period of time. Some stood up. DocKnow headed at a very fast pace for the too many hot peppers room. Others made fresh coffee and Crystal Mare meticulously brewed her green tea.

Fifteen minutes later, they all sat.

DocKnow asked, "any comments?"

A long silence ensued as if everyone had drifted into their own personal reality in search of their own experiences.

Walks with Woman said, "these experiences seem to have a tinge of intuition in the sense the guidance or sense of knowing to do the unusual is like a small gap in time that opens and closes quickly."

Tom said, "this has a sense of stepping between or in and out of different worlds or dimensions of reality. It reminds me of a game I played with my own mind. I place something in a specific place and sense energetically that something is slightly different. Later, when I returned to get it, it is not there even though I know I had put it there. In another time, the items appears in the exact spot I had originally left it. Recently, I realized that my energy is different in these different moments; and I have wondered if I have been crossing vibrational dimensions or entering different energetic aspects of myself."

DocKnow asked, "what if everything that has been said is true. We have experienced liminal spaces through meditations, ceremonies, etc. What if there is a refined aspect of energetic vibrations that enable and creates different perceptual capacities of what is real?"

Crystal Mare noted, "it means that everything is energy and different frequencies create different realities. It also means that as we become more consciously aware of the presence of what is present, we carry a higher vibration and therefore experience reality deeper, more fully, and with oneness."

"In a sense," said Tom, "this means that when asynchronous experiences occur, they may be of a higher frequency that we cannot understand or perceive until our vibration or conscious awareness increases. Hence, presence increases our capacity to access the asynchronous like strange attractors that lead to synchronic moments. There is no causality, only attracting frequencies that can manifest the resonance of our perceptual reality."

DocKnow chided, "that is a massive leap of integrative energies that accurately reflects the emerging and evolving consciousness of awakening. As energy beings evolve through releasing old beliefs, or programming, if you prefer, the higher our frequency the less lower frequency perceptions and beliefs remain. They dissolve like eliminating old code. "

White Horse noted, this reflects David R. Hawkins stages of consciousness[5]. He indicated that higher frequencies elevate awareness and lead to the complete dissolution of beliefs that carry lower frequencies such as greed anger, etc.

Walks with Woman said, "isn't that what is happening. The ascending energies prophesized by the Mayans and others says that the frequencies of the earth and the increasing conscious awareness is leading to higher vibrations. Thus, we are dissolving lower frequency thought patterns such as shame, humiliation, greed, anger and fear for courage, self-determination and development of internal authority."

DocKnow agreed and said, "the higher vibrations are higher frequencies of conscious awareness as depicted in Tom's diagrams. It is not often understood that thoughts have a specific frequency and pattern that remains the same until the frequency increases through conscious awareness and a deep experience of the presence of what is present."

"Whoa!" exclaimed Tom. "it just sunk into me that each thought is energy and therefore has a frequency. It just clicked that these are feeling tones often referred to in different spiritual teachings. Change the frequency and the tone changes and therefore the thought or feeling changes."

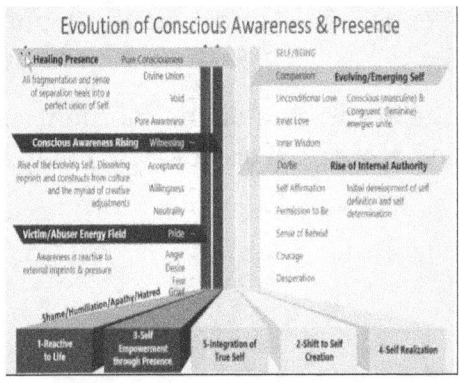

"WHOA!" said Crystal Mare. "This suggests that energy precedes thought and feeling, and that we generally do not pay attention to energy. Instead, we focus on the feeling tone to create the thought and behavior. Change the feeling tone to neutral as done when fully present, the behavior becomes simply witnessing and experiencing the presence of what is present without reaction."

DocKnow smiled and said, "it seems we are experiencing what has been held as asynchronous information that has been floating in the background awaiting a higher frequency of awareness to trigger the resonance needing to bring forward the deeper and more integrative awarenesses."

Tom added, "in my terms, the veil of the mind has lifted to reveal the established energies holding our awareness in a specific set of emotional and feeling tones. Freed from these established and lower tones, we are realizing an entirely new awareness of the presence of what has always been present. This deepens my understanding of the diagram as each stage of development is the establishment of higher tones that elevate and bring into awareness new awareness until we reach the highest levels of presence whether we call it healing presence, pure love, God, or creation. In a sense, our development is an ascension to higher feeling tones as if we are reprogramming ourselves or rewriting the musical score of who we are. In terms of vertical development stages or stages of conscious awareness, a new feeling tone permeates one's experience and therefore one's felt sense of existence."

Everyone sat in the emptiness of the moment as if a blank slate had been provided before each created their own new world.

FOUR: ASSEMBLAGE POINTS

The group broke up for lunch, which ended up being for the day. Tom decided to walk to the medicine wheel. As he approached, DocKnow was waiting at the thirteen moon wheel.

Teasing DocKnow said, "fancy seeing you here."

Tom laughed and said, "I can say the same thing about you being here."

"I suppose," said DocKnow, "this morning's conversation has you wondering about something on the edge of awareness."

Tom smiled.

"And" continued DocKnow, "you followed that wondering to the medicine wheel."

"There is something about feeling tones" said Tom, "that has to do with being in one's center and is somehow related to Castaneda's assemblage points."

DocKnow and Tom stood looking at the wheel, then slowly meandering around it for over half an hour, neither speaking.

After a while, Tom said, "I am going to walk over to the original medicine wheel."

DocKnow nodded and the two walked over to the other medicine wheel.

As they approached, Tom said, "it seems the assemblage point as discussed by Castenada is like being centered in the medicine wheel and therefore centered in oneself."

DocKnow added, "that is true, and it has been widely used for many diagnostic processes for various health issues. However, I sense that is not what you are alluding to.[6]"

Tom said, "our conversation reminded me that Castenada referred to the capacity to shift or redirect the focus of the assemblage point could lead to the ability to perceive different dimensions and to reveal that reality as we perceive it is predetermined by our programming or feeling tones. In some way, we arrive with a preconceived program of the types of experiences we seek when entering the physical body. The program is likely preconceived ways of perceiving the world as a means to experience very specific events and behaviors. This is why he called it the assemblage point. It is where all of the energies to create the body and our programming converge to create our human experience."

"And" said DocKnow.

"And" said Tom, "the assumption that we are not programmed for specific experiences is the concept of free will. It is believed that free will means creative control. However, the programming allows choices within the range of perceptions until we garner more conscious awareness and shift the feeling tones, thereby dissipating the existing programming. This leads to becoming aware of the presence of what is present and leads to vertical development and rising through the stages of conscious awareness."

DocKnow asked, "do you remember the images of the assemblage point you seen in the past?"

"Of course," said Tom.

"As you reflect on them, what stands out the most?"

Tom said, "according to the images, the assemblage point reveals or reflects the auric field surrounding the human body. OMG! It is through the assemblage point that the human body and therefore human energy is in constant creation as it moves through the assemblage point. The assemblage point is the point of human creation of ourself in all forms including our physical programming, and all beliefs, assumptions, and perceptions."

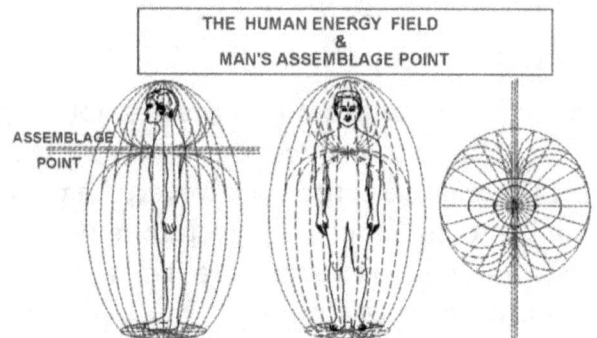

https://upload.wikimedia.org/wikipedia/commons/c/c6/AP-Fig1.jpg

"And" said DocKnow.

"And" said Tom, "I need to take a break."

They walked back to the farm without talking aloud while a whole lot of activity was going on inside Tom's head.

When they arrived at the farm, Tom went straight to his room and opened his computer graphics program. He was having images flying through his third eye that he wanted to capture.

FIVE: RE-MEMBERING

For most of the evening and well into the night Tom rotated between creating images and researching everything he had ever had in terms of books and articles. Carlos Castenada, A. H. Almass, Jon Whale. At some point in time or dimension, he realized that for the many years he had collected, read, and stored information that now was revealing itself especially about the assemblage point.

As he scanned the different images and advocacies, he realized that he was focused on the inter and multidimensional aspects of the assemblage point. He wondered, 'is it possible that the assemblage point is the defining assemblage of oneself, including the physical manifestation as described by Castenada. Is it possible that this is the focal point of the third eye and multidimensional experiences.'[7]

Scanning the image in his mind, he suddenly startled himself with the realization that he had been utilizing the assemblage point in a variety of ways though unconsciously.

Castenada had said the assemblage point was directly between the shoulder blades. Like stepping into a liminal time and place, Tom realized that when invoking the medicine wheel to support healing moments frozen in time, he had placed his left hand over the assemblage point and supported moving the person into a liminal state, one where they could witness, recall and release the explosive energies held the moment frozen in time. He watched the many people that he had worked with him shiver and release the energies, less or no longer wounded and able to live more fully in the moment.

He recalled the exact spot between his shoulder blades, for much of his awakening period of life, he had felt massive pain at the assemblage point. He recalled thinking, 'I wish someone would hit me hard directly in that spot to release the pain.' Tonight, he recalled that Castenada had referred to the shaman's blow to the assemblage point as a way to restore stability and clarity to the person.[8]

This led to another memory where Tom had blown his breath across the chest at the area of the assemblage point during healings with clients. In a subtle shift, the client revealed they felt something had cleared and they felt more like themselves.

He then moved into a liminal state and watched himself using circle selenite disks during his own meditation especially when the assemblage point was aching. He focused his attention on clearing, centering, and stabilizing.

He watched himself sharing different stone slabs, often agate, with the healing den classes with the primary placement to have the person lie on the slab between their shoulder blades.

Finally, he recalled at different times when his assemblage point was especially active and painful, he had worn a selenite pendant on his back as if to draw out the pain creating energies.

He realized now it may have been intent and focus that supported the easing of the pain and now even more so wondered about the clearing effect of the selenite. He assumed it was both....all matter is energy directed into form.

As he finished watching these memories on his eyelids, he felt a massive energy shift as if he had clicked energetically deeper into himself.

SIX: ASSEMBLING

Tom woke the next morning realizing that he had stayed up most of the night trying to crystallizes his understanding of the assemblage point. Very groggy, he crawled out of bed, headed for the shower, and hopefully would clear his head.

As the cob-webs cleared inside his head, his mind sharpened. He realized he had gotten so focused on trying to diagram the assemblage points, or more accurately, the functioning of the assemblage points that he had gone into a highly focused liminal space. Now, he wondered if he had created anything that made sense. He also realized that he had had a large integrative liminal experience.

"Coffee," muffled through the door interrupted his thoughts.

"Please," Tom responded as he got from the shower, dried, dressed and walked out the bathroom, smelling fresh and feeling old.

Close by Crystal Mare stood with a very large coffee for Tom and her own large brewed with song green tea. Tom grabbed at the coffee as Crystal Mare pulled it back to get his attention.

"I would like a moment to chat when you feel coherent enough to hear about my meditation with assemblage points," said Crystal Mare.

Tom was connecting deep into the eyes of Crystal Mare as he said, "yes, of course, let me get a quart of the black magic elixir in me and then we can go for a walk and talk."

Tom sat at the kitchen table and ate a piece of bear claw that was suspiciously sitting on the table untouched. He wondered if it was laced with some magical cinnamon as he was suddenly crystal clear and deeply present. He filled the large mug with more Gevalia French Roast coffee and walked out the door with Crystal Mare.

As they walked outside, the light was a bright silvery color. Everything seemed illuminated. The moon was massive as if he could reach up and touch it. He looked at Crystal Mare who mischievously smiled and said, "it's three am."

Tom thought, 'no worries. I feel completely rested' and then he concluded the coffee, and the Danish must have been bathed in Crystal Mare's magical singing. 'No wonder I feel so good.'

They found a couple of trees with chairs facing the moon. Sat down and filled themselves with the silence, then with the radiating luminosity of the moon.

Like a pebble thrown into a lake under a full moon, Crystal Mare said, "I have experimented with assemblage points during meditations at different times. Last night or more likely early this morning, I decided to do meditation with the focus on the assemblage point.

Tom looked attentively as if to say, 'go on.'

Crystal Mare continued as if in a trance reliving the experience. "I seem to be re-membering as it felt perfectly natural to set the focus and intention first on the assemblage point and second to focus on clearing the programming of what was creating this reality and be open to a broader experience. When I did this I felt an immediate connection with the assemblage point and quickly connected with my Heart and solar plexus. My Heart flooded with energy. I moved my focus into the solar plexus and began a scan from the left side (of my solar plexus) to the right. A burning energy occurred as if something was releasing or maybe awakening before releasing. Then I experienced multiple images, showing up of people in my life and how they are elevating at this time and what they are releasing. Several beings arrived deep in my subconscious and appeared to be going through some sort of manual that was downloading into my being."

She continued, "then I began having physical kriyas[9] that included rocking from left to right and then from front to back for an extended period of time. A lot of heat and energy was flowing from my root chakra down my left leg into my foot. I noted that when this occurred, our most gentle kitten Iona came and laid on my legs. I Saw many images, including a faraway city that appeared to be lit up with violet blue-ish energy. It appeared to be off my upper left. I finished curious and refreshed."

After a long pause, Tom said, "what would support you in this moment."

Crystal Mare said, "I guess I needed someone to hear and validate the experience in some way."

Tom pondered then said, "come join us" as DocKnow walked towards them with coffee.

Surprisingly, this did not affect Crystal Mare.

When DocKnow sat down, and nodded to continue, Tom said, "I have several responses. First, yay! Clearly an impactful experience. Second, I have had similar experiences when working with meditation and the assemblage point. Third, I wonder how you are experiencing and or making meaning of the meditation. Energetically it feels multidimensional, possibly without clear focus and intent except to explore or be open to the experience."

Crystal Mare choked on her green tea creating a perfect imitation of DocKnow spewing liquid over everyone.

DocKnow and Tom both laughed and settled quickly into their

chairs.

Crystal Mare said, "I choked as I had all of those reflections and now realize that if I have more clarity in my intention and focus, then I might be able to explore the presence of what is present in any of these dimensions."

She paused and added, "this reminds me of the discipline required to do out of body experiences and lucid dreaming."

Surprised and supportive, both DocKnow and Tom nodded agreement.

Crystal Mare shifted the conversation and asked Tom, "what were you doing last night? The energy from your area filled the house. Now I wonder if it had an impact on my meditation?"

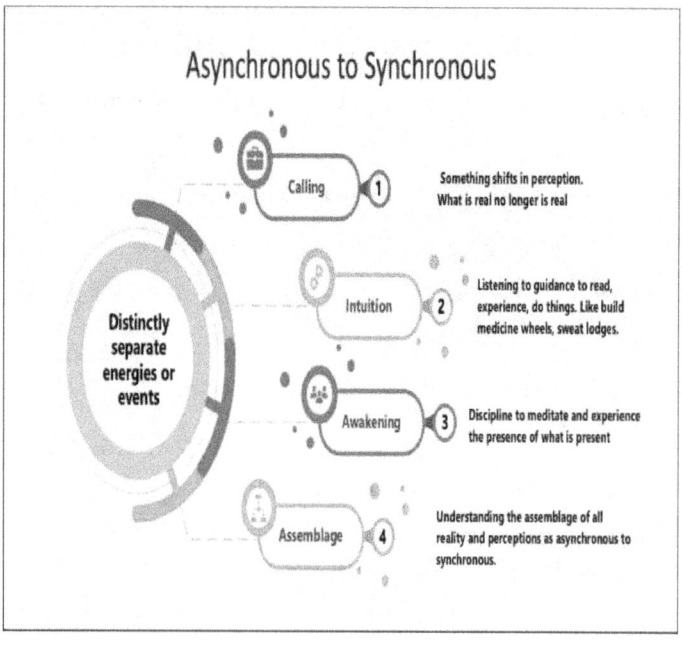

DocKnow answered, "he was experiencing the slinky effect where his understanding was finally catching up with all of his indelible moments or if you prefer asynchronous moments that were slowly coming together through synchronicity to expand his conscious awareness.

Wisely, Tom said, "what he said."

After an ancient minute, DocKnow added, "much of life is lived as if it is logical, sequential and causal. In truth it is mostly asynchronous. Some events seem paradoxical in that they do not fit anywhere into our logical view of life and yet they carry a resonance that is higher than day to day life. This resonance or energetic footprint remains in our auric field waiting for the overall vibration of the person to reach resonance with these experiences. When resonance is attained, a massive awareness permeates the person as happened last night with both of you. What seemed paradoxical and asynchronous becomes synchronistic . Synchronicity elevates the awareness of the presence of what is present. The asynchronous moments are brought together through the holistic and evolving energies found in liminal spaces. Perception gathers depth and breadth unseen before as it requires the resonance creating higher vibrations of awareness."

Tom thought about what DocKnow was saying and suggested "let's take a used coffee and tea break while I get something."

All nodded and they headed into the house as they turned to see the sun rising.

SEVEN: INTEGRATING

As they entered the house, they found White Horse and Walks with Woman heading out to the barn to feed the animals. Shortly later, Walks Softly arrived almost as quietly as his name.

The house became alive with excitement as DocKnow seemed like he had drunk some Red Bull on top of all the coffee. As it stands, it was one of his happy fits that every once in a while would fill him like a hot fudge Sunday with whip cream and a cherry on top.

As he danced around the house, breakfast magically appeared, the animals were fed, and every sat in a state of grace for the blessings of each other and a glorious day.

During breakfast, everyone was sharing their experiences from the night before from dreams to screams to dancing memes as it seems the conversation on assemblage points had stirred everyone in some form or fashion.

When everyone felt like they had a shared glimpsed of each other, Tom said, "I want to share a few things I was working on in the ethereal spaces of last night."

He reached into his satchel and passed out a diagram and said, "I was trying to capture what I was understanding about assemblage points. I came to a phrase that assemblage points are the constellation of oneself."

Everyone did a coordinated heads-down moment to their copy. As everyone scanned, Tom noticed that the energies were rising in terms of frequency and for him a sense of heat. He looked around and everyone was extremely focused on the image and energy emanating from the presence of what was present.

Tom said, "it might help to consider the image as an echo that starts as pure energy that begins to lower its vibration and therefore its frequency. The assemblage point when constellated in a specific frequency, say each of you as you are presently as a human being, is a frequency that formulates into a blueprint or program of who you are, followed by the next lowering frequency of forming into a body and person, followed by a potential to be just as you are absorbing the imprints of family, culture and society. For some the potential continues as the frequency begins to reverse through the evolving and emerging self that hears the call to awaken."

Tom paused.

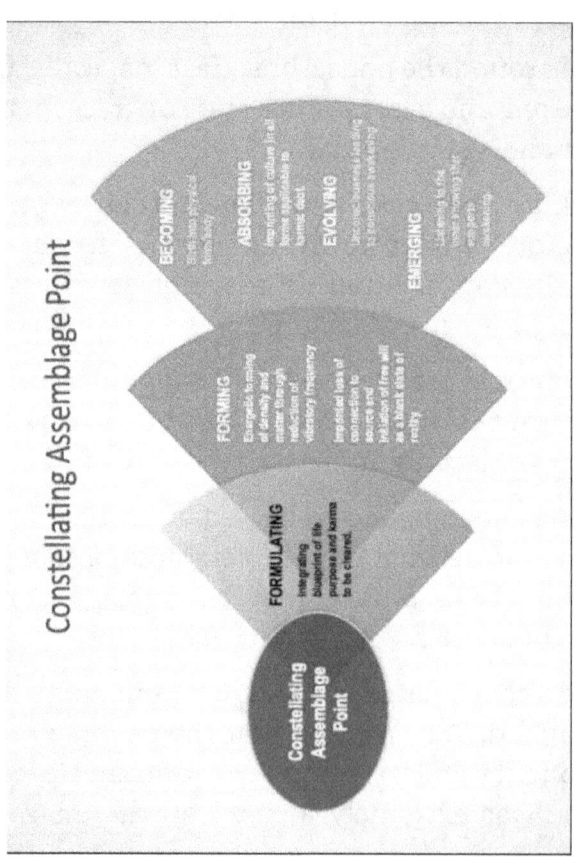

As everyone seemed to glean then deepen their sense of understanding, Tom continued, "the diagram is meant to reflect the shifting or lowering of the vibrations until density (formation of matter) occurs. The end result is that the human energy field becoming physical with the constant flow of the energy through the assemblage point. We typically call it the aura without focusing on how the energy field is actually in a state of flux like a 360 degree infinity loop. "

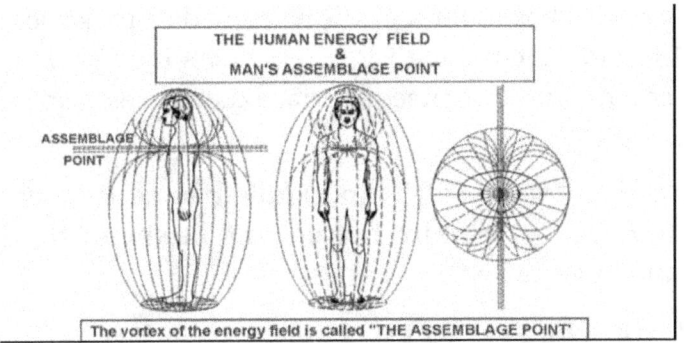

White Horse said, "this explains 'free will' as the ultimate form of choice to experience whatever you wish, however within the confines of your constellating assemblage point. Which is another way of saying the internal program impacted by karma, culture, etc. and the redetermined purpose for choosing this life. Hence,

DocKnow said, "I could see how this is confusing. If I follow the echo to the forming of matter, the human body, mind and emotions, through lowering the vibrations, then in the last echo, a choice point can occur where the calling to awaken occurs that may or may not be accepted. The evolving and emerging self as a form of awakening is not everyone's choice. It might be that they choose to continue in the present state of experiences."

Tom nodded and said, "is that not what is happening in the present global conflict over power, religion, politics, and wealth?'

A long pause.....like infinite silence that will remain empty or fill with insight.

White Horse said, "this explains 'free will' as the ultimate form of choice to experience whatever you wish, however within the confines of your constellating assemblage point. Which is another way of saying the internal program impacted by karma, culture, etc. and the redetermined purpose for choosing this life. Hence, it may be some people's journey to experience authoritarian rule while other might choose to awaken democracy."

"Walks Softly said, "this might seem like a diversion, but it seems your prior diagrams of the path to self-awareness seem to be in the last fan shape suggesting that an awakening process is possible, but not destined for each person."

The others nodded agreement.

Tom was pleased as his integration seemed to make sense to the others. He said, "I agree with White Horse's insight that free will is about choice and the consequential experiences associated with those choices."

Tom turned to Walks Softly and smiled as he reached into his satchel and said, "you means these?" And he shared the diagrams from prior conversations.

Crystal Mare said, "so every person has a purpose which ultimately is about having new experiences which might include being able to clear karmic obligations or simply to experience the polar opposite of our other lifetimes, like changing roles from victim to perpetrator and vice versus or from husband to wife, etc.. This means that that for some their purpose is to awaken, which explains the spiritual phrase 'remember to not forget'. In other words, we do not remember our existence outside of this present experience when we come into this world. The awakening process is like a calling of hints to remember. Some will hear the calling and see conscious awareness[10]. Others will not. Both are perfect."

Tom looked at DocKnow and smiled. They nodded to each other.

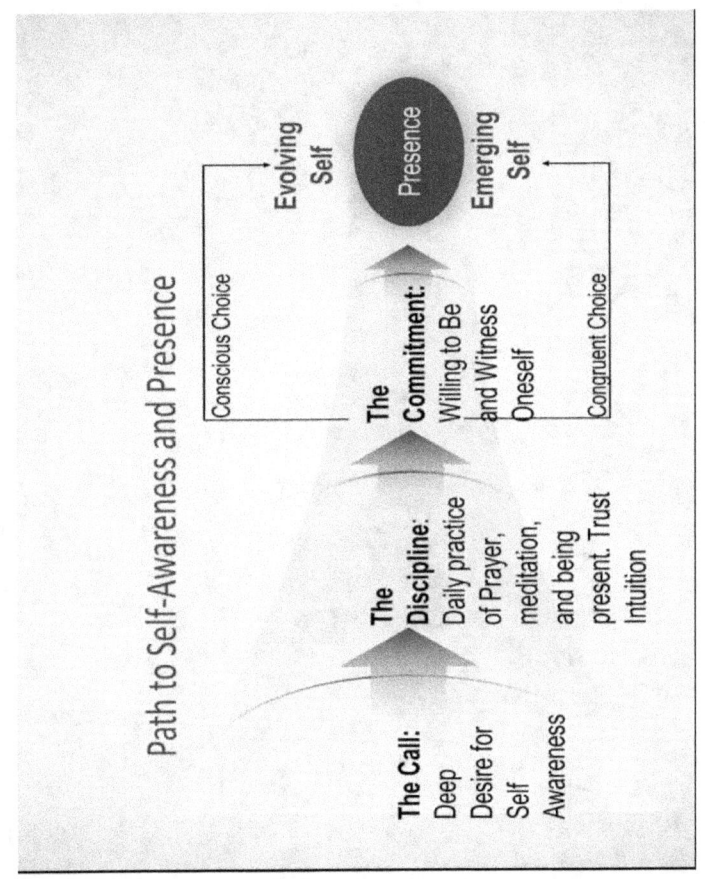

Path to Self-Awareness and Presence

The Call: Deep Desire for Self Awareness

The Discipline: Daily practice of Prayer, meditation, and being present. Trust Intuition

The Commitment: Willing to Be and Witness Oneself

Conscious Choice

Congruent Choice

Evolving Self

Emerging Self

Presence

Emerging from Congruent Choice

Walks with Woman suggested they take a break. All agreed.

There was a slightly faster than a walk move towards the bathrooms while a few headed for the nearest tree.

They decided to break for lunch to allow everything to simmer.

EIGHT: FURTHER INTEGRATION

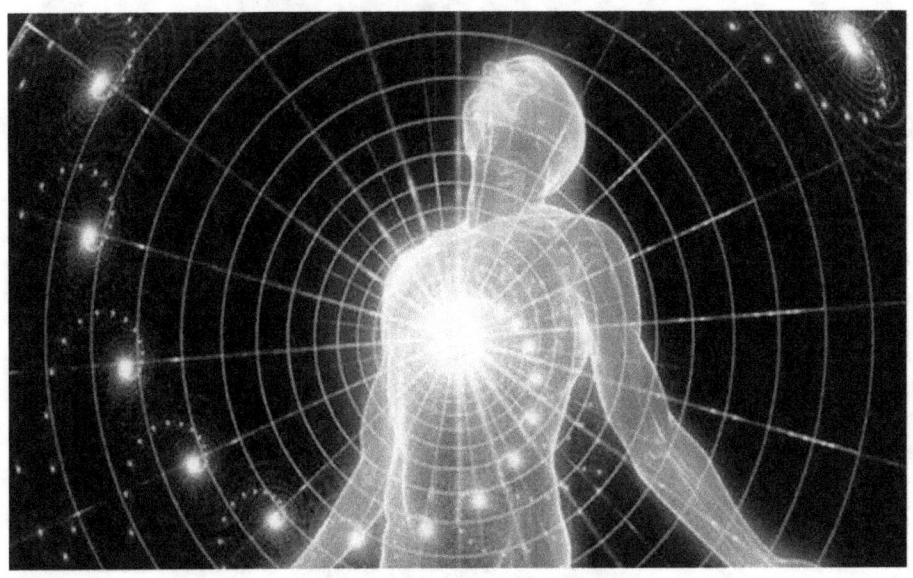

When they returned, Tom asked if they would like to go the next step or as he rephrased it, to look at the next diagram.

All nodded.

Tom continued. "The second diagram depicts the entropic energy echo in the sense that it reflects the unconscious formulating, forming and becoming of existence with little self-awareness beyond day to day life. As we have discussed, it is the habitualized life from living through pre-programing and external authority."

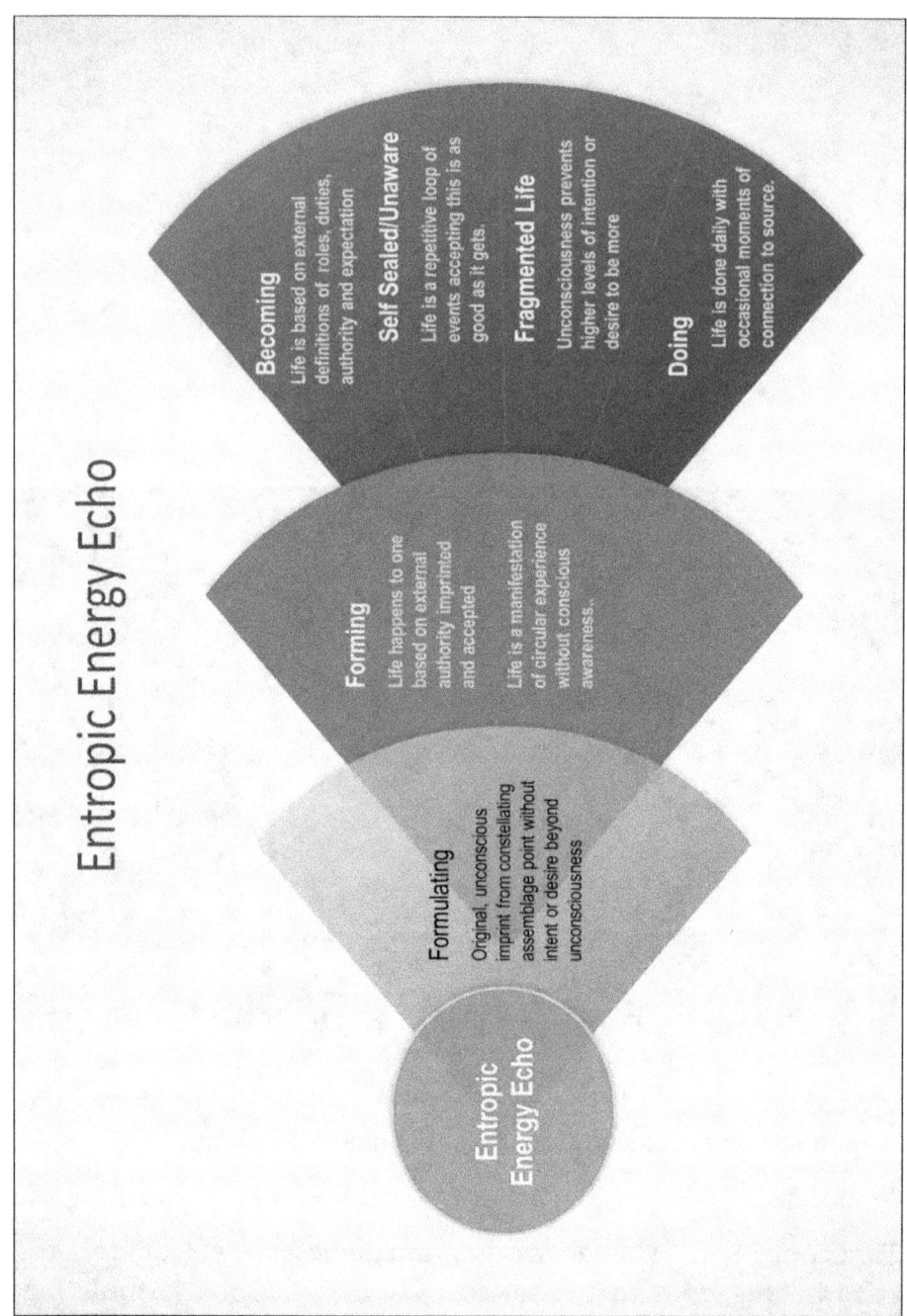

Entropic Energy Echo

Becoming
Life is based on external definitions of roles, duties, authority and expectation

Self Sealed/Unaware
Life is a repetitive loop of events accepting this is as good as it gets.

Fragmented Life
Unconsciousness prevents higher levels of intention or desire to be more

Doing
Life is done daily with occasional moments of connection to source.

Forming
Life happens to one based on external authority imprinted and accepted

Life is a manifestation of circular experience without conscious awareness..

Formulating
Original, unconscious imprint from constellating assemblage point without intent or desire beyond unconsciousness

Entropic Energy Echo

Everyone focused their attention on the diagram while the energy of the group began to rise as if the vibrations were seeking a higher frequency and therefore a higher level of awareness.

DocKnow suggested, "consider this… the person who has chosen to live a very specific life, unaware of other choices and has settled into what life has presented as what is possible and normal."

"That said," noted White Horse, "it is the person whose purpose from this life is to experience to the fullest the typical birth to death experience."

"The syntropic energy echo in the formation of the assemblage point," said Tom, "is activated beyond a habitualized existence when the calling to awaken is heard and accepted."

This directed everyone's attention to the third diagram.

DocKnow noted, "syntropy is the infinite potential that we create through awareness of the felt sense of a desired reality. Most called it the understanding of manifestation. In physical existence, everything moves slower due to lower vibrations, however when we have a clear felt sense such as love, it emanates outward to others."

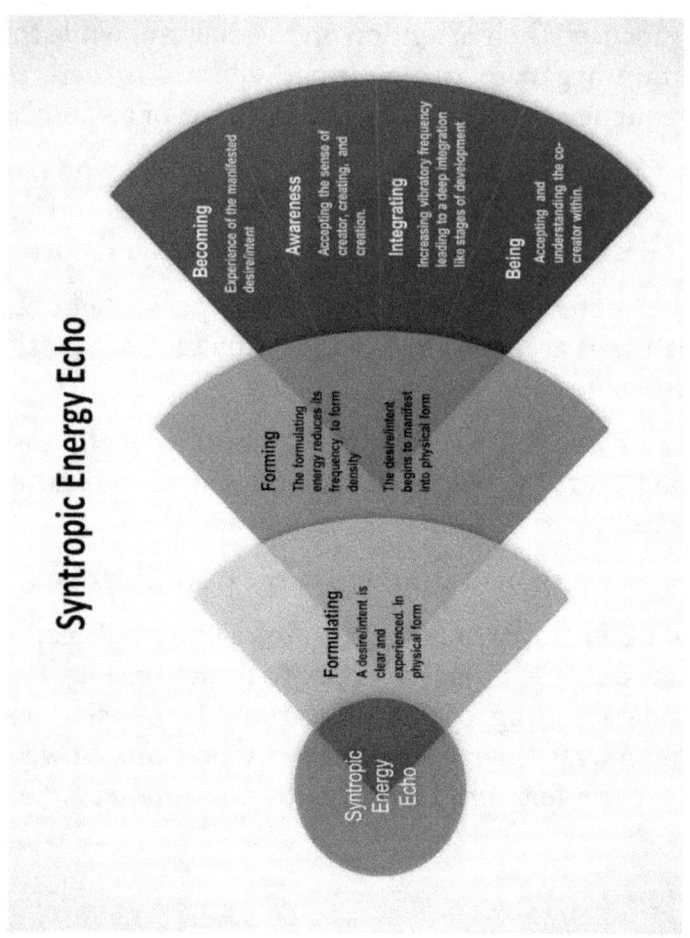

Walks Softly noted, "I know this sounds like redundancy, this seems to be leading us towards more of the diagrams from our prior conversations. The only difference is we are more consciously aware and seemed to be able to hold higher vibrations. Hence, our understanding seems deeper, wider, more filling. We seem to be in a creative infinity loop of dissipation and creation."

All the others agreed.

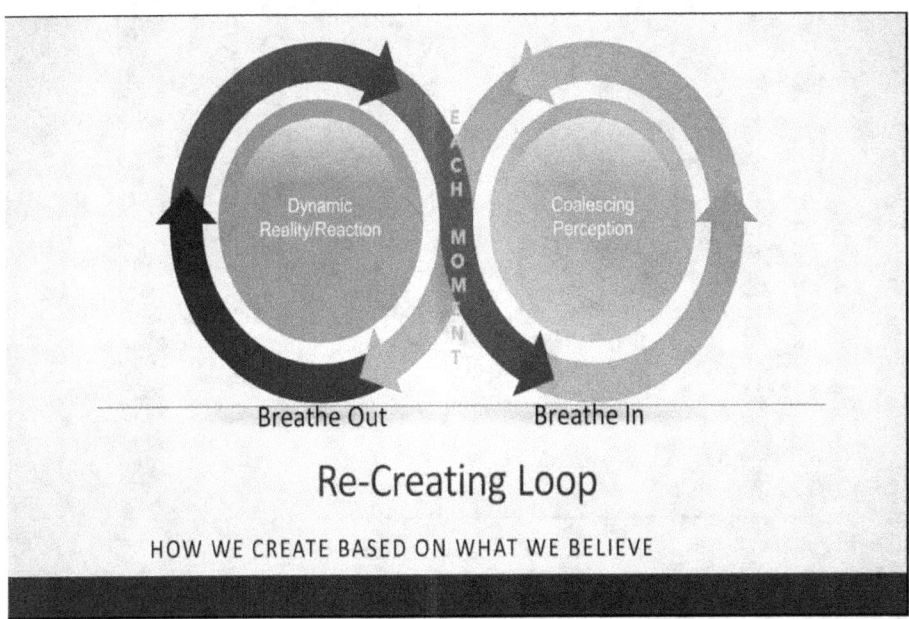

Re-Creating Loop

HOW WE CREATE BASED ON WHAT WE BELIEVE

Tom nodded to DocKnow who reached into the satchel and brought out the diagrams from prior conversations and shared them with the group.

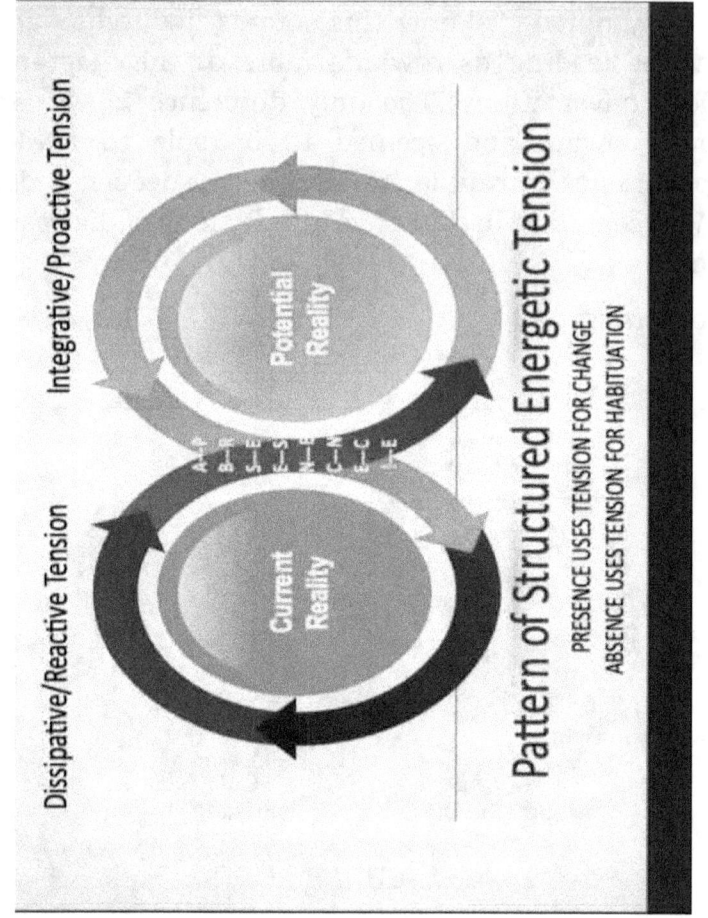

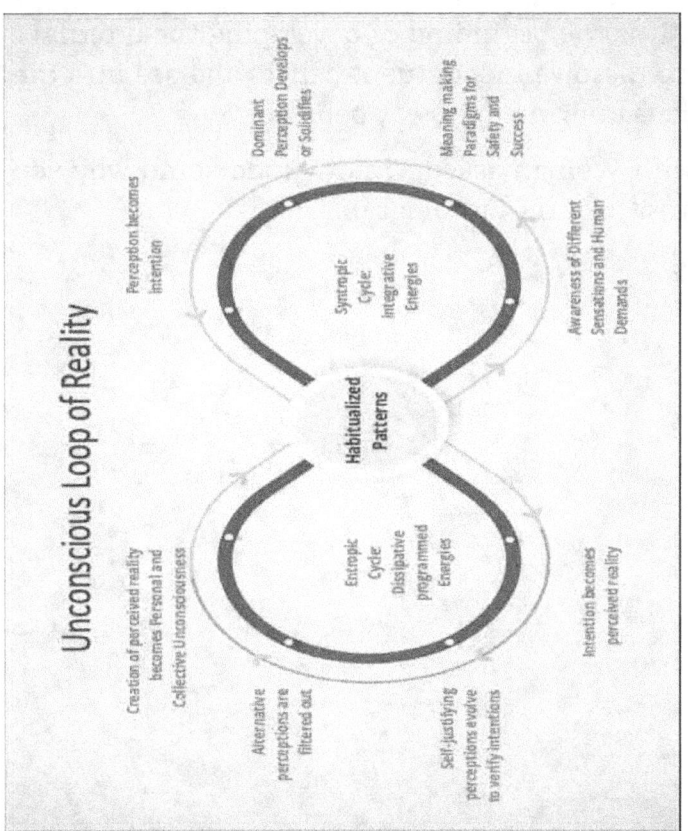

Tom said, "it does not take too much of a stretch to see that the entropic/syntropic process is constantly moving through the assemblage point, perpetuating programmed and habitualized perceptions."

Crystal Mare added, "it also reflects that when one heeds the call to awaken, the syntropic process emerges. In other words , entropic energy can be self-perpetuating of the existing accepted patterns, or it can become evolving which then supports the emerging creative aspects of syntropy. In essence it reflects the processes required for the evolving and emerging self through conscious awareness of the presence of what is present."

"Heeding the call" said DocKnow as everyone nodded. "The awakening process dissolves the preprogramming and imprinted beliefs of culture so that conscious awareness can begin to develop. It is the beginning of developing the internal authority needed to dissolve incongruent beliefs and see into the truth of false beliefs imprinted to sway behavior."

Walks with Woman asked, "I now understand why you used an Ouroboros[11] for the last diagram."

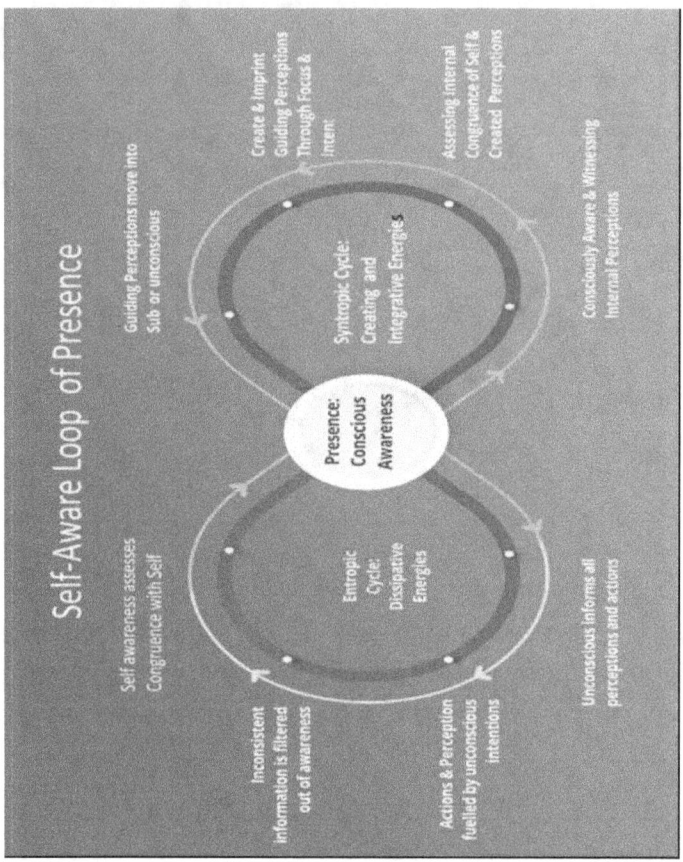

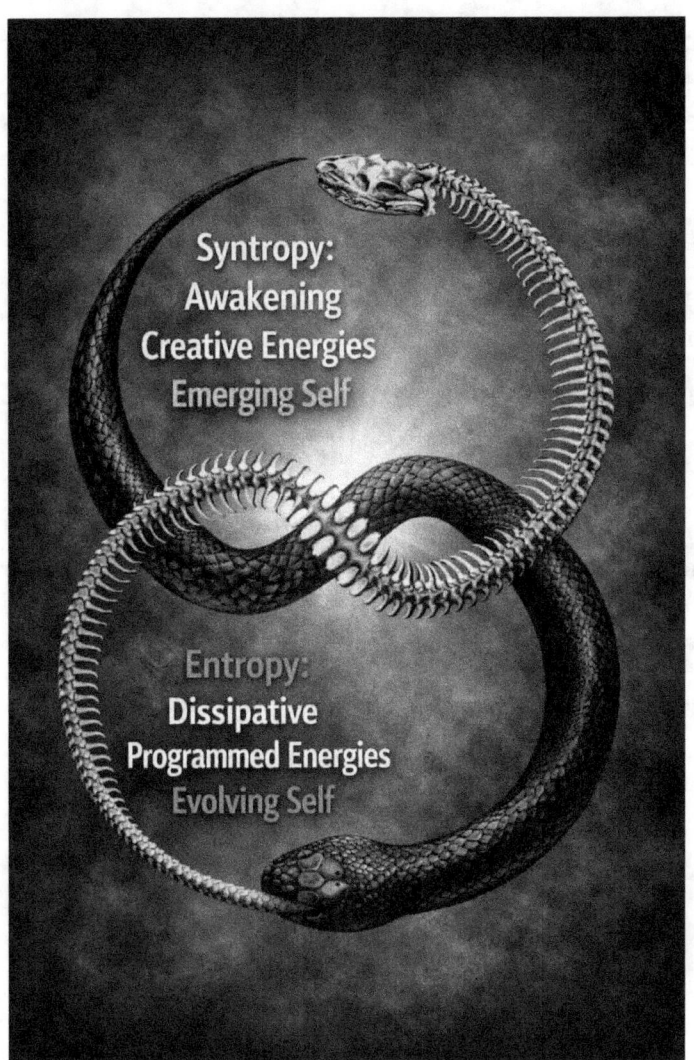

Tom smiled, "are we not constructing and deconstructing ourselves on a moment to moment basis. The Ouroboros holds the assemblage point and therefore the point of our existence in human form. As we develop more conscious awareness of the presence of what is present, we realize we are only limited by our own beliefs and perceptions."

White noted, "so the ouroboros is a mythical image of the impermanence as well as constant creation of life?"

DocKnow smiled and said, "yes, it is."

DocKnow looked around and said let's take a break for the day. This is a lot of information that requires studying the diagrams more than just seeing the images and the words, but to allow the frequency of the concepts to permeate at a deeper level, possibly triggering even greater insight and awareness."

No one moved as if already in that deep state of embodying the presence of what is present.

NINE:
PERMUTATIONS[12]

The next morning, Tom was up and raring to go... he did not know where. He felt like he was on the edge of something. Maybe a discovery. Maybe on the edge of himself. He decided to sit on the edge between anxiety and excitement rather than allow his 'monkey mind' to create many stories.

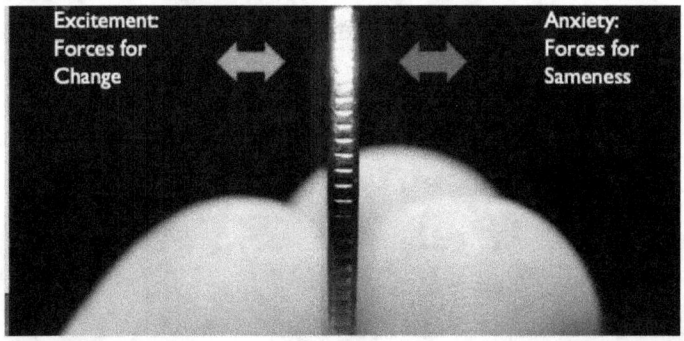

He knew that when he felt this way, he was caught between old beliefs about something new or surfacing. Occasionally he would get very excited and other times he would get anxious. If he was not able to sit in the tension, he would play ping-pong with himself bouncing between memories and dreams. He knew better and decided to just sit and witness the energy, possibly discover the felt sense that was seeking conscious awareness.

As he made coffee, Walks Softly came into the kitchen. He nodded to Tom as they both got their gigundus mugs of coffee and sat down.

Walks Softly asked, "I have been pondering most of the night about 'free will' and something about the 'monkey mind'. Would you be interested in chatting about it?"

Tom smiled, "I have been having my own version of the same topic. What or where do you want to start?"

Walks Softly said, "if I understood everything, we are programmed prior to coming into human form, hence, we are all spiritual beings. We come into physical form with a specific purpose to clear karma, which generally is created through mental or emotional attachments[13] or to experience very specific aspects of being human. Where we get lost is through 'free will'. Even though we have the ability to choose our lives, we are generally preprogrammed to learn specific lessons including clearing karma. These lessons can be like emotional or mental traps if we are fully present to ourself and able to witness beyond the immediacy of the moment and the programming. So, in a way, we are set-up to struggle."

Tom nodded to go ahead.

Walks Softly continued, "is it a set-up?"

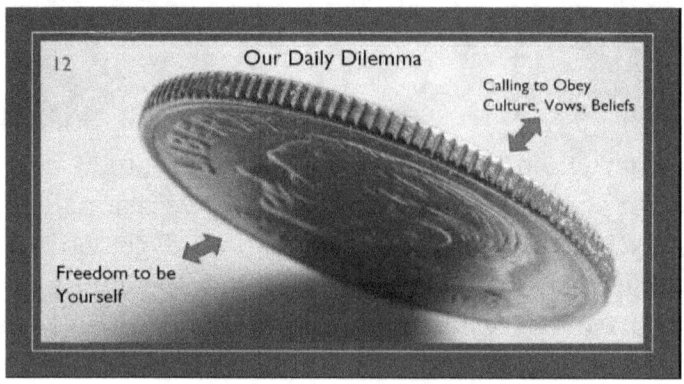

Tom smiled as DocKnow joined and said "it is if you are attached to the idea that it's a set-up. It isn't if you realize that it is simply an encouragement or test, if you prefer, to be more present."

Walks Softly seemed to be reeling inside himself as if a multitude of permutations were going through his mind.

Tom said, "what if you stop thinking to understand and simply sit here until you have a felt sense of the energetic conflict, probably countervailing beliefs based on imprints or experiences from the past. For example, I was sitting here realizing that I was playing ping pong with myself as it can only happen in our minds. I decided to stop the thoughts and sit between the anxiety and excitement of the energies to see what surfaced."

Walks Softly had a moment as his eyes flashed recognition. He said, "just listening to you seemed to shift my vibration and as I felt it rise, the confusion diminished, and I began to witness myself. As a witness, the felt sense revealed that I was holding onto a limited view of 'free will' and choice. I was attached to believing that my life has not been filled with free will as many choices did not feel possible. Then I heard a loud knowing *"says who,"* and realized I was living under the pretense of external authority. That realization released the confusion and sense of contradiction. I understand the concept of programmed assemblage point, now. And it does not matter if I was imprinted or preprogrammed, I have the free will ergo choice to dissolve it."

DocKnow shifted the conversation slightly, "I had not thought about the monkey mind as permutations of thoughts seeking a resolution to an internal conflict. It makes me realize that the intent is to create a feeling of understanding or maybe safety in what I know. Thanks guys, I will enjoy sitting on the edge of this awareness to see what surfaces."

Tom and Walks Softly were a bit surprised by DocKnow's pronouncement, then realized that it was a deep insight each of them could use.

Shortly thereafter, the house became a buzz of doors opening and closing as people woke, showered, headed for the kitchen or barn and the day-to-day began.

TEN: FREE WILL

After a bonus wakeup meal of breakfast burritos, DocKnow Style[14], all cottage cheese, milk, and cream cheese were cleaned out.

"Guess we will need a grocery run" said, DocKnow with a big smile.

After clearing the table, scraping the dishes before dropping them into the dishwasher, and brewing two pots of coffee and a teapot of green tea, they moved outside.

The air was brisk, low forties, and it took about a minute for everyone to turn back to the house to grab jackets and a few blankets. It looked like a poorly orchestrated snake dance.

When all settled, jackets on and lap blankets tucked in, Walks Softly shared a bit of the early morning discussion and added, "I would like to chat about free will and how monkey mind is a series of thought permutations seeking understanding with existing beliefs or a desire to feel safe."

Everyone looked at Walks Softly and one by one nodded their support.

Crystal Mare asked, "can we start with how thought permutations can become ping pong?"

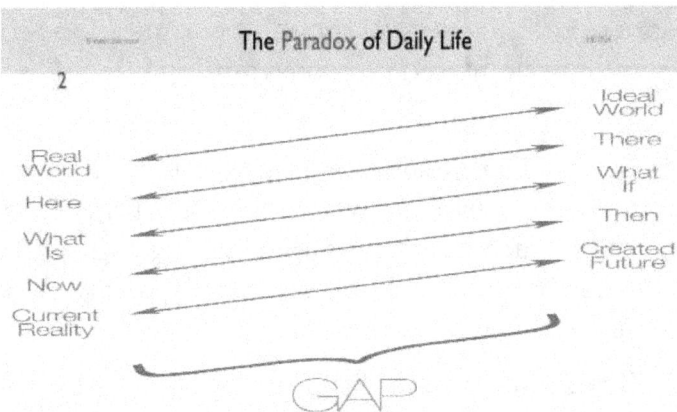

DocKnow said, "let's start by looking at how ping actually occurs" as he handed an image to everyone.

After ample time to get the gist of the image, DocKnow continued, "the image suggests that in a daily act to understand or to fit something into a safe concept, we bounce back and forth between the two poles. If we make it ping pong the poles would be the past and the future, so we would bounce between memory and ideal, past there and future there, What was and what if, past then and future then, and feared or frozen reality and created or potential reality."

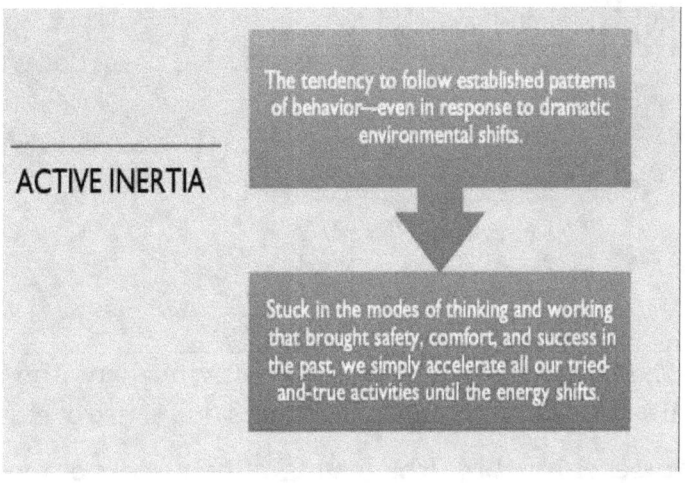

Crystal Mare said, "these are all thought permutations controlled by the assemblage point and its programming."

"Yes" said Tom. "The illusion of free will is that we can freely move through these permutations as if we are fully present, when free will requires an understanding of the process and capacity to witness and discern what is real or true before making any decisions We are stuck on active inertia."

"Woooo," filled the air from multiple sources.

Walks Softly asked, "so the awakening process is what begins the process of true 'free will'?"

Everyone nodded as if a common moment had occurred.

DocKnow added, "you might wonder why there is not more awakening or clearing of the assemblage point so that more conscious awareness is possible?"

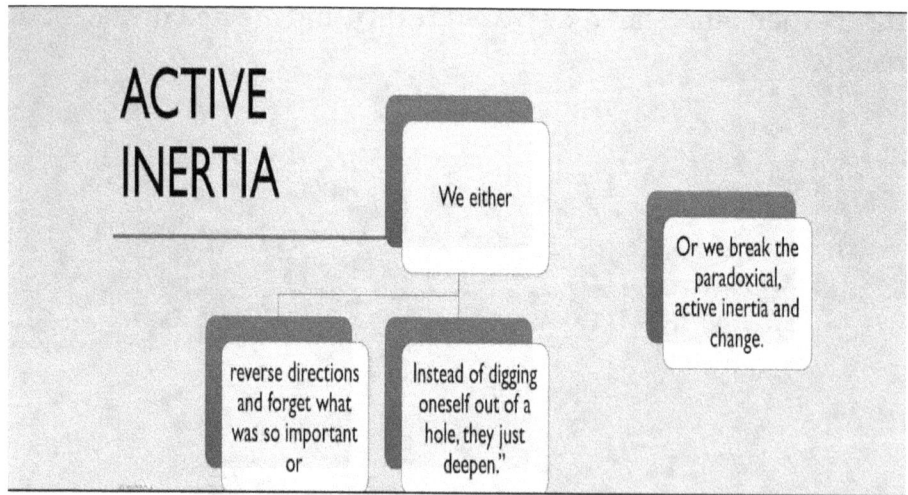

Crystal Mare said, "because we are convinced of the identity within the assemblage point, it threatens our sense of existence."

White Horse, chimed in, "the feeling of being lost or disoriented arises when you lose your sense of identity, your sense of who you are. Every time your assemblage point shifts from its customary place, you are letting go of who you have taken yourself to be."

DocKnow nodded and continued, "as Castenada indicated any shift in the assemblage point brings with it a sense of difficulty and anxiety, and there are many ways that this is experienced."

Tom added, "I imagine it can be experienced like a mid-life correction where one feels that, "I am lost. I don't know what to do. I don't know which way to go. I don't know which direction to take, and I feel disoriented and unoriented. I have no purpose or clarity."

DocKnow continued, "one's sense of self is being in touch with the flow of presence. In disorientation, what is really lost is this sense of being who you are via an internal roadmap that suggests what to do and which direction to take. It is the deprogramming of the assemblage point through an increase in frequency and what one if able to perceive that leads to the identity crisis."

Tom added, "without understanding the depth and breadth of the presence of what is present through conscious awareness of to what you are attending, the delusion (preprogramming within the assemblage point) rises, you believe it, and this, in conjunction with the loss of one's sense of Being, leads to this sense of bewilderment.

It can be difficult to apply this understanding to practical action in the world until one begins to develop the evolving and emerging self. It is in becoming able to witness oneself through thoughts, feelings, and actions. This means until the calling is heeded to move towards conscious awareness, the established assemblage point prevents the pursuit and perspective most readily seen through inner experience such as meditation."

Walks with Woman said, "the assemblage point creates a sense knowing what is supposed to happen in a concrete situation, such as turning on the heat when cold or working for a certain amount of income to cover your monthly expenses."

Tom nodded and added, "however, when you are dealing with the unfoldment of the presence of what is present, you need to remember don Juan's response to Castaneda's question, 'What should I do? don Juan said, 'Nothing.' We need to understand the significance of the insight that nothing needs to be done in order to facilitate our unfoldment, except surrender to the call to awaken one moment at a time to the presence of what is present."

White Horse noted, "one of the ways I have revealed my active inertia is to ask a series of questions during meditation. Typically, I focus on only one as each seems to have a hidden insight that reveals itself over time. The key is to not expect an obvious answer. In other words, do as Castenada suggested, do nothing as you wait in silence and be open to surprise. Otherwise, you will get an already programmed answer from the assemblage point program."

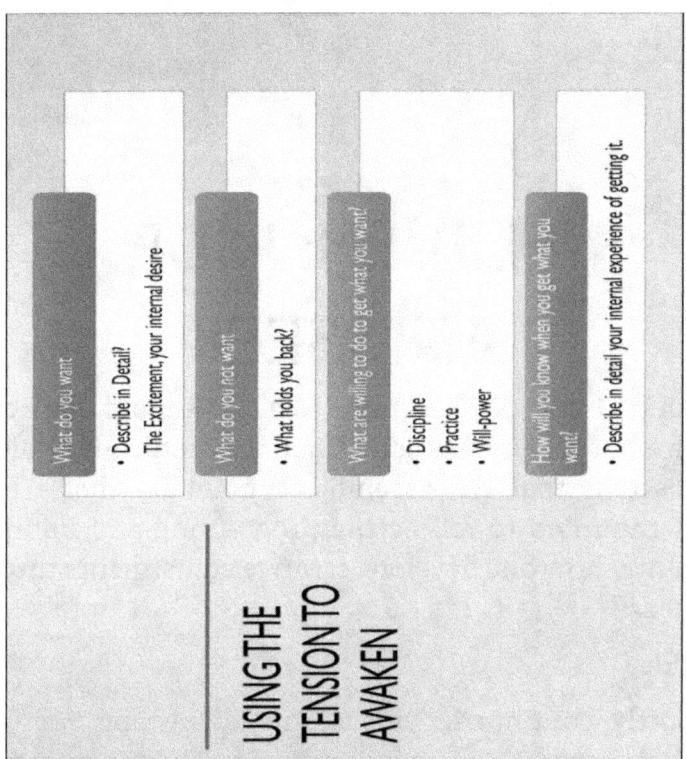

USING THE
TENSION TO
AWAKEN

What do you want:
- Describe in Detail?
  The Excitement, your internal desire

What do you not want:
- What holds you back?

What are willing to do to get what you want?
- Discipline
- Practice
- Will-power

How will you know when you get what you want?
- Describe in detail your internal experience of getting it.

ELEVEN: HIDE AND SEEK

The group took a bio-break which should be called a replenishment of caffeine rush. When they returned, Walks Softly said, "it seems that the assemblage point is what triggers or activates the mind to follow the programing and imprints and subsequently how one develops creative adjustments through life experiences."

Tom nodded.

Walks Softly continued, "this seems to be how we establish our relationship with external authority. The programming and imprints are energetic perceptions of how to make meaning. These then filter other options from awareness. In other words, unless internal authority is preprogrammed, the awakening process of shifting the assemblage point is the beginning of conscious awareness and the development of internal authority."

DocKnow added, "it is also the beginning of conscious awareness of the presence of what is present. We begin to dissolve or see beyond the imprints and programming as if a spark of awareness permeates our experience."

Walks with Woman said, "this feels like we are playing hide and seek with ourselves."

All laughed and nodded in agreement.

Walks Softly noted, "this feels like a spiritual hide and seek in the sense that the goal is not to pursue or to find something hidden, it is to become aware of what is. And this type of hide and seek has a completely different felt sense."

White Horse said, "I agree, it is, and it isn't. "

Everyone looked at White Horse with a suspicious eye to see if he was teasing.

White Horse chuckled and said, "the evolving self does require learning how to witness oneself so as to reveal the imprints from family, society, culture that lead to beliefs as well as to whatever programming might be within the assemblage point. So, in away we are playing hide and seek. The emerging self is surrendering to the presence of what is present, so it is the allowing in of the true self or if you prefer, it is discovering reality through surrender, that is, through allowing the presence of what is present in."

The group was silent as they felt the depth of what had been said.

Crystal Mare said, "so the human mind is really our constructed prison here because it remains within the influence of the assemblage point until we begin to develop conscious awareness. There are no physical shackles preventing us from achieving whatever we want to achieve except the self-imposed limitations of what and how we perceive clearly influenced by our social and family systems."

DocKnow reminded everyone, "we literally can only see what we believe. If the assemblage point focuses our beliefs and perceptions then we cannot see a reality beyond them until the awakening process occurs."

Tom said, "so the calling is an evolutionary process to remember to see beyond the constraints of external authority and the begin to develop a path to evolve which then frees the emerging self."

DocKnow said, "some would describe what we say is as the unfoldment of the assemblage point."

Walks with Woman responded, "So our focus is to find a way of seeing the unfoldment, understanding the unfoldment, facilitating the unfoldment, and surrendering to the unfoldment.

This sounds like learning to witness and stay present."

DocKnow added, "Surrendering to the unfoldment becomes freedom of movement of the assemblage point and you become aware that freedom is a matter of surrendering to the spirit that is moving you, your emerging self."

Tom added, "as we unfold the assemblage point, it seems that life, our life, tends to thrive on going with the flow. Everything just feels right and ideas flow to and from you as if the path lights up for you[15]."

Crystal Mare noted, "it seems that the assemblage point tends to house the fear, worry, and lower emotional vibrations. These desperate thoughts are what detain us until we are able to realize they are only thoughts and not facts. When we begin to focus on our inner world and inner states through meditations, we begin to focus our attention wholeheartedly on being present to what we are attending to and we begin to dissolve the programming and the assemblage point unfolds."

TWELVE: A WALK TO UNFOLD

"Seems like a good time to take a break and then go for a silent walk," said Crystal Mare.

The group nodded and after refreshing themselves with releasing and loading up on liquids, they walked towards the woods across the pasture.

It was like a dark well filled with the silence of many decades of neglect. Tom felt like his heart or assemblage point was opening as he was not so sure which anymore.

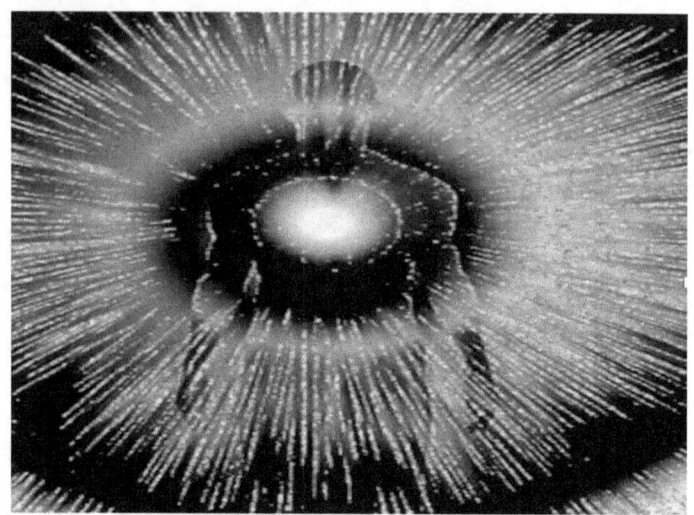

He looked around and sensed a deep radiance from everyone.

DocKnow said, "just breathe and bask in the energy."

Tom noticed that it felt like a deeper sense of liminal space. They walked until dark then returned to the farm for dinner and sleep.

THIRTEEN: INTENT AND DESIRE

The next morning, everyone was alive and awake at daybreak.

There was laughing and lively chatter until the sun broke through and everyone moved outside to watch the unfoldment of a new day. It was not lost on them that they were watching a mirror of their own daily unfoldment.

Shortly afterwards, someone said, "let's get some breakfast!"

All walked into the house feeling vibrant.

After breakfast, Tom asked "can we chat about how desire and intent fit into the awakening or unfoldment process. It seems that desire can be active or passive, or maybe assertive from beliefs versus receptive from surrendering?'

All nodded as they cleared the dishes, cleaned the kitchen and refreshed themselves with coffee, tea or milk.

They formed in the living room where Crystal Mare had lit a fire.

She smiled as everyone walked in and said, "I am chilled, and I really love a fire."

Tom chuckled…and said, "she really LOVES a fire".

As they settled into the circle of sofas and chairs facing the fire, DocKnow said, "desire and intent play a major roll in awakening and the unfoldment process."

He paused as everyone allowed themselves to begin to focus their attention on the topic and not the cozy fire.

"Desire" said DocKnow "can be an intense energy that seeks satisfaction,[16] or it can be experienced as something already satisfied. It can become an obsession, or something ignored. For example, the desire to learn can be a process of chasing information to be smarter than anyone else or it can be a process that comes from a sense of knowing to be still to see what emerges.[17]"

DocKnow continued, "intent[18] can be unconscious or conscious as well as high vibration or low vibration. Often, the intent is based on false assumptions or beliefs which has led to such phrases as 'the road to hell is filled with good intentions'. Generally, intention is dictated for many by their core assumptions, beliefs and assemblage point programming that leads to reactions instead of centered responses. "

Crystal Mare said, "it seems the call to awaken is both an unconscious and conscious desire. For me, I was unconscious as the sense of being more than I was or how I saw the world. As I answered the call by paying more attention to what I was paying attention to, I became more conscious of the desire to awaken. This led to an intention to meditate daily."

White Horse added, "following her statements, intent can be like the phrase to *'remember to not forget'* to wake up' though I suspect that this is more unconscious. Yet, there does seem to be a driving energy to become more conscious or to unfold."

Tom asked, "is it possible that desire can be a motivating energy like wishful thinking and a state of mind that actually manifests reality? If we stay with our conversations the last week or so, it seems that desire can be drive one to collect material items often referred to as the 'good life' so it becomes a yearning of sorts; however, from a syntropic perspective where desire is the energy and acceptance of an unfolding reality, it becomes the forming aspect of one's reality whether it is physical, spiritual, or mental. For example, when I felt as if I was already living on the farm, it became a clear path to purchase and ownership."

Tom continued, "the felt sense of a desire is the manifestation of a new reality. Is that not what happens with each unfolding awareness of a deeper, unseen till now, insight or epiphany or shift into liminal space? Each holds the allowing in, surrender, to the desire for conscious awareness without any programs or external authority to indicate what or how it should be."

Walks with Woman said, "so in our state of attending to the presence of what is present our own unfolding occurs. Our intent is focused on the presence of what is present which enables old programs to dissolve, beliefs and imprints to be dissolved and to remember we are a spiritual being seeking not only a physical experience but to embody the spiritual being."

"Kind of like," said Walks Softly, "living in naked awareness by having the courage and compassion to be fully engaged with the presence of what is present completely unaware of what will appear in each moment and knowing we are safely embodied."

"I could not have said it any better," said DocKnow.

All nodded.

FOURTEEN: TIME CRYSTALS

After a short break, they moved outside as the sun had warmed the outside air. A circle was formed around the patio table with massive mugs of hot beverage. Crystal Mare managed to bring along several blankets to replace the warm fire.

Walks Softly asked, "so how do the time crystals, the moments frozen in time, fit into assemblage points?"

"Good question!" roared from several people.

DocKnow laughed, "seems we have a lot of pent up energy based on your energetic response."

"Maybe, it is in response to the cold air," smiled Crystal Mare as she pulled another blanket around her shoulders.

Everyone smiled as they noticed that the sun was warm, and the air was quite cool at 55 degrees Fahrenheit.

Walks Softly asked Crystal Mare, "can I have one of those blankets?"

After feigning 'no' she flung one across the table covering DocKnow, Tom, and Walks Softly. All laughed.

"Time crystal are moments frozen in time," said DocKnow. "Once formed, they can become constellated with similar energies to form a large constellation or cluster of time crystals."

DocKnow paused then said, "let's try something new. Let's do a guided meditation."

Everyone liked the idea and nodded agreement.

DocKnow had them close their eyes and begin to breathe slowly to a count of five, pause, then breathe out to a count of five. He continued this process as everyone settled deep into their bodies while the frequency began to shift. Images appeared on their eyelids; some call it their third eye. As if from a faraway place, DocKnow's voice created a deep resonance that seemed to create common images for everyone. Angelic harps were in the distance as everyone seemed to travel deep into some galactic place.

Image by image followed DocKnow's voice.

Suppose we are like Stars....a collection of energetic Experiences Floating in Our Awareness

Some Experiences Shine Bright and Create Constellations of Memories

Suppose We are an Energetic Collection of Experiences that form our true sense of self

Suppose as we integrate all our energetic experiences, our core sense of self Grows

We become a divine shining light of conscious awareness.

What if Unfinished, unsatisfactory or incomplete energetic experiences do not shine bright

What if Unfinished experiences become free floating, as if frozen in time and space without the ability to shine again or to be integrated in conscious awareness. They lose life force.

What if they Float until touched by conscious awareness through healing presence that rejuvenates and frees the Energetic experience to be integrated.

What if
Surrounded by
Traumatic energies
that remain in
unconsciousness,
the time crystal
floats as an
unfinished
and wounded
energy triggered
by unintegrated
memories.

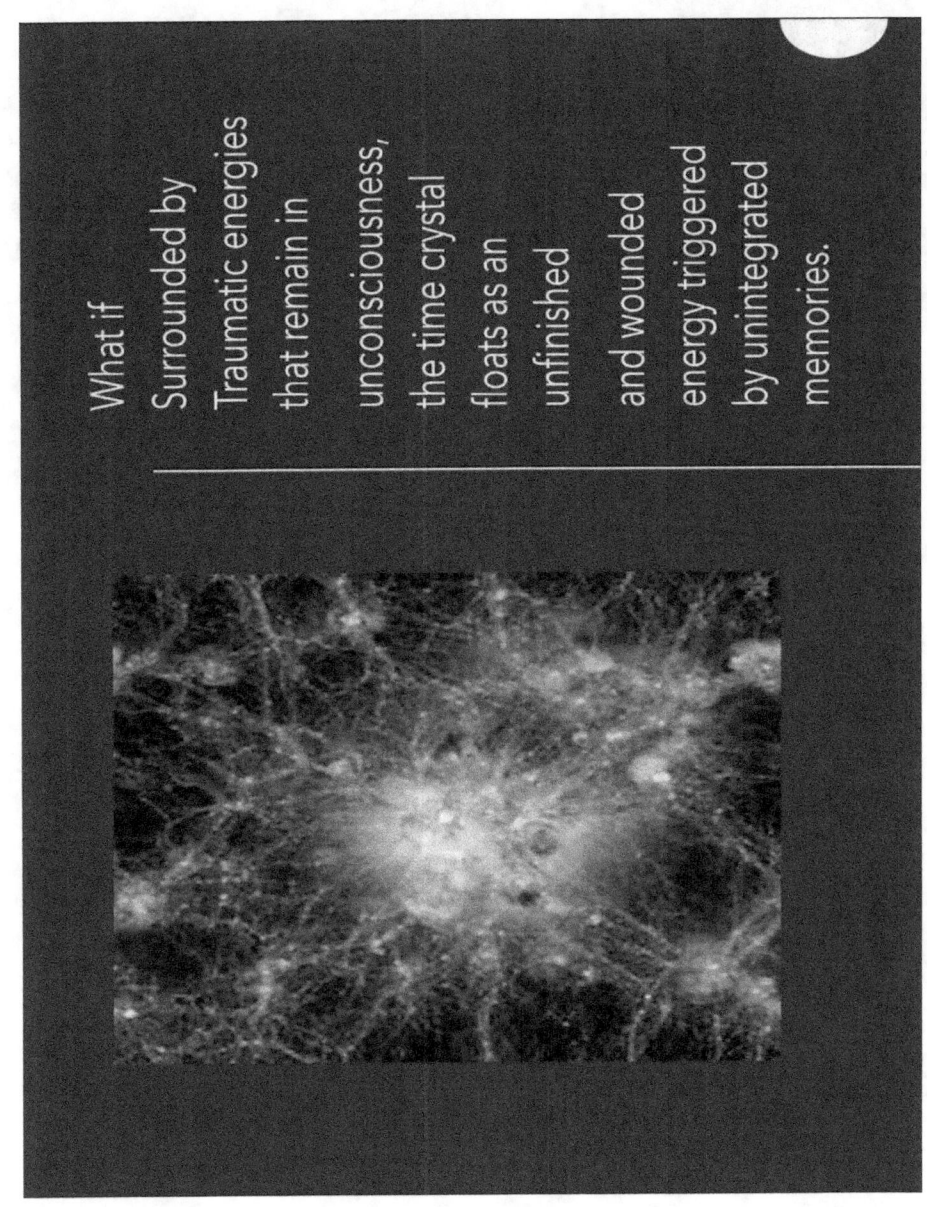

What if These frozen moments are paradoxically guarded by the traumatic energies.

What if Presence releases
the energetic guardians
of the trauma

What if the guardians
dissolve with
the Trauma, a healing
presence enables
Completion of the.
The integration of the
unfinished experience

What if Releasing
Frozen Moments
in Time/Place
Creates Wholeness

Presence Returns One
To Conscious Awareness
And sense of wholeness

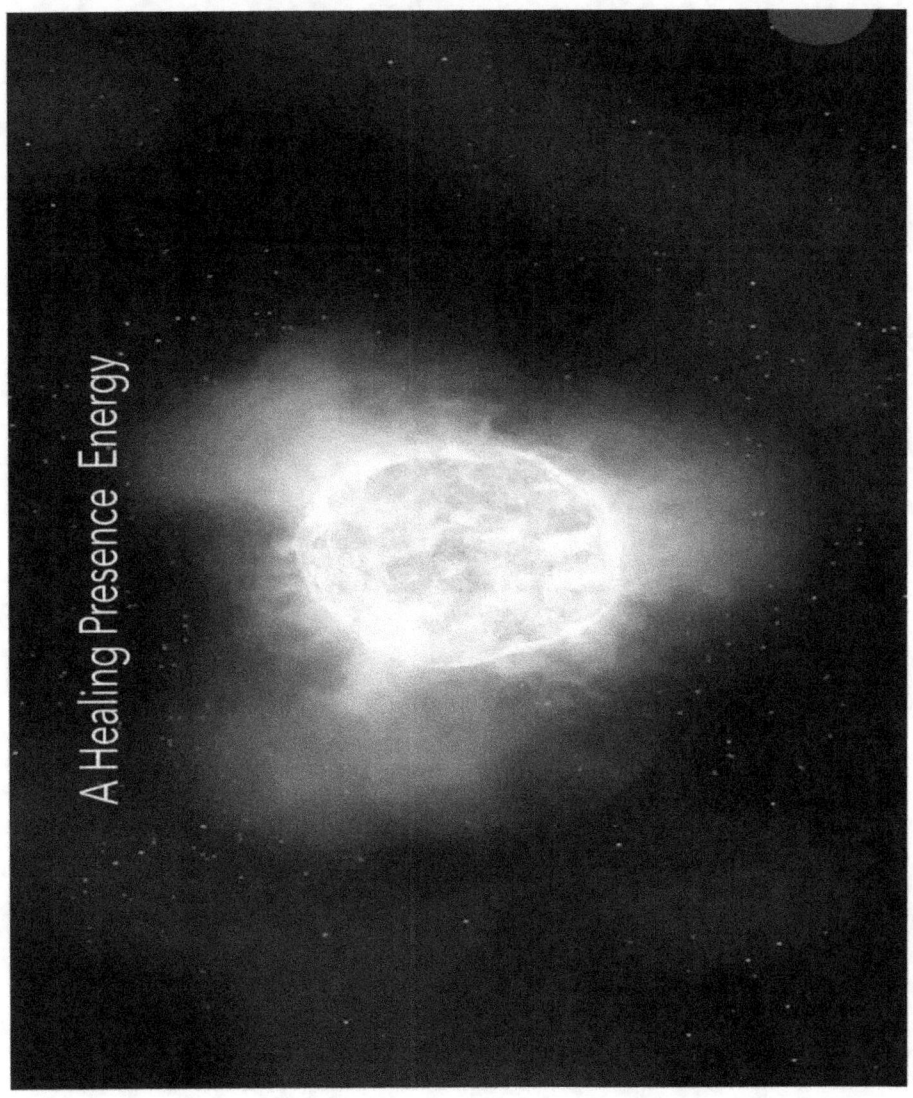

A Healing Presence Energy

In what seemed like a timeless moment, DocKnow's voice came more into focus as the images faded. "wiggle your toes and your fingers," said DocKnow as he supported everyone to come fully into their bodies.

"Feel yourself here in this moment as you open your eyes" guided DocKnow.

Everyone seemed between excited and wondering what had happened.

Tom chuckled to himself as he realized DocKnow had shifted everyone into liminal space where knowing becomes the form of learning.

FIFTEEN: CLARITY

When the group reformed, DocKnow asked, "can you see that the frozen moments in time, the time crystals are floating in the auric field?"

Heads nodded

"Does it make sense that the time crystals as well as all experiences are part of the collective energetic experience of the individual that are made meaning via the assemblage point?" he continued.

Tom added, "so as we awaken, the evolving self slowly dissolves the time crystals and likely shift the programming of the assemblage point, while the emerging self enables the true self, free of programming and imprints, to begin to completely clear the assemblage point of karma and other constrictions."

"Precisely" said DocKnow.

It was obvious to everyone that the guided meditation had cleared something for each of them and opened a deeper understanding of the assemblage point and time crystals. Now, each realized it will take time to understand exactly what they understood.

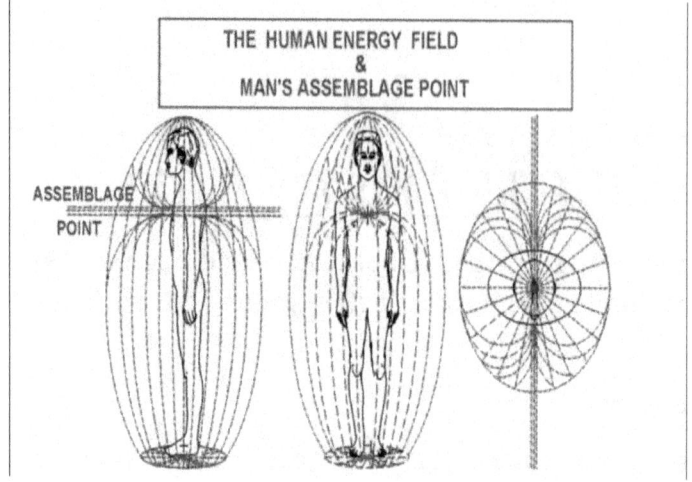

https://upload.wikimedia.org/wikipedia/commons/c/c6/AP-Fig1.jpg

[1] Carlos Castaneda (December 25, 1925[nb 1] – April 27, 1998) was an American anthropologist and writer. Starting in 1968, Castaneda published a series of books that describe a training in shamanism that he received under the tutelage of a Yaqui "Man of Knowledge" named don Juan Matus. Wikipedia

[2] https://www.carlos-castaneda.com/

[3] *Asynchronous:* two or more objects or events) not existing or happening at the same time.

[4] You could think of the mind as a field: Whatever you do and think—all of the actions that will lead to happiness or suffering—are like seeds or imprints that you plant in it. When conditions are ripe, a seed will sprout into an experience. Trinlay Tulku Rinpoche, "The Seeds of Life"

[5] The Map of Consciousness Explained: A Proven Energy Scale to Actualize Your Ultimate Potential

[6] Jon Whale https://whalemedical.com/ the Naked Spirit and the Catalyst of Power

[7] **The Assemblage Point: The Nexus of Perception**
The assemblage point is central to Castaneda's teachings; it is a bright spot inside our energy structure that serves as the pivot point of our perception. Something so far away from our daily lives and abstract makes it difficult to comprehend.
Imagine a radiant egg, a cocoon of light, around your physical form. A plethora of energetic strands, brimming with potential, make up this cocoon. Imagine a spot inside the egg where these threads meet to form a sensory hub. This is where everything comes together; it's the prism through which we view the immense energy field around us.

The Assemblage Point is not static. Every time it moves, shifts, or realigns, our view of the world changes. It's like we're switching between several realities, each with its own distinct point of view. Castaneda provides an even more detailed description of the assembly point in his subsequent writings. According to him, it's a collection of energy fields that sits just behind the shoulder blades and is roughly the size of a tennis ball. Readers interested in developing their own energy bodies will find this explanation to be a useful starting point.

Castaneda, C. (1968). *The Teachings of Don Juan: A Yaqui Way of Knowledge.* Touchstone/Simon & Schuster

https://subtle.energy/mysteries-of-perception-carlos-castaneda-and-the-enigmatic-assemblage-point/?utm_source=Subtle.Energy&utm_campaign=153f0e16e6-EMAIL_CAMPAIGN_2024_08_03_04_57&utm_medium=email&utm_term=0_-153f0e16e6-%5BLIST_EMAIL_ID%5D&goal=0_d05f2db778-153f0e16e6-228528674&mc_cid=153f0e16e6&mc_eid=d5e6a22413

[8] Native medicine men can shift Assemblage Points with a single blow, catching their apprentices by surprise. The Shaman fixes the direction and location of the shift using his 'unbending intent'. These types of shifting techniques although effective and spectacular are not suitable for clinical work. They are too abrupt and require too much personal energy and self-discipline to be effective. In a clinical setting patients frequently have a low location and poor health. In such cases a softer approach, using the special techniques such as breath with clearly focused intent.

[9] Kriyas are physical and spiritual cleansing practices that yogis have used for thousands of years in both the Hatha and Kundalini yoga lineages. And now, these ancient techniques are starting to become popular among yoga practitioners in the western world also.

In yoga, the meaning behind the Kriyas is to move and awaken potent energy to create a physical, psychological, and spiritual shift in our being. You do this by performing specific exercises (Kriyas) that combine repetitive movements and mantras, creating a moving meditation.

The Sanskrit word Kriya translates to action or effort, and Kriya yoga is often called the "Yoga of Action or Purification." Each practice helps to cleanse the body and reduce common ailments and illnesses. Other benefits include boosting energy levels and stimulating digestion.

Kriya yoga also increases life force and strengthens the energetic body in preparation for a spiritual awakening.

https://theyogatique.com/what-are-kriyas/#kriyas-definition-yoga

[10] Children are taught to question and challenge in ways that are good for dharma. Buddhadharma goes deeper when you question. Value comes from challenging and investigating. Kyabgön Phakchok Rinpoche, "Keys to Happiness"

[11] Ouroboros Ou·ro·bo·ros ˌyu̇r-ō-ˈbȯr-əs   a circular symbol that depicts a snake or dragon devouring its own tail and that is used especially to represent the eternal cycle of destruction and rebirth

2 usually ouroboros or less commonly uroboros : something (such as a never-ending cycle) that is likened to or suggestive of the Ouroboros symbol

Trauma is a time traveller, an ouroboros that reaches back and devours everything that came before Junot Díaz https://www.merriam-webster.com/dictionary/Ouroboros

[12] permutation (noun); permutations (plural noun) a way, especially one of several possible variations, in which a set or number of things can be ordered or arranged: "his thoughts raced ahead to fifty different permutations of what he must do"

[13] Our journey is about being more deeply involved in life and yet, less attached to it. Ram Dass

[14] Many flaming peppers and chilis.

[15] Dotts, Richard. Come and Sit with Me: How to Desire Nothing and Manifest Everything . Richard Dotts. Kindle Edition

[16] a strong feeling of wanting to have something or wishing for something to happen:

[17] Learning or knowing is often jaded by the educational system that uses reward/punishment as the system of measuring what one has retained instead of what and how one has learned.

[18] a strong feeling of wanting to have something or wishing for something to happen, resolved or determined to do (something, giving all your attention to something

www.ingramcontent.com/pod-product-compliance
Lightning Source LLC
Chambersburg PA
CBHW070348130626
46556CB00007B/3073